MISSED-UNDERSTANDING

SHORT LOVE STORIES

SACHIN C NARWADIYA

Made with ♥ on the Notion Press Platform
www.notionpress.com

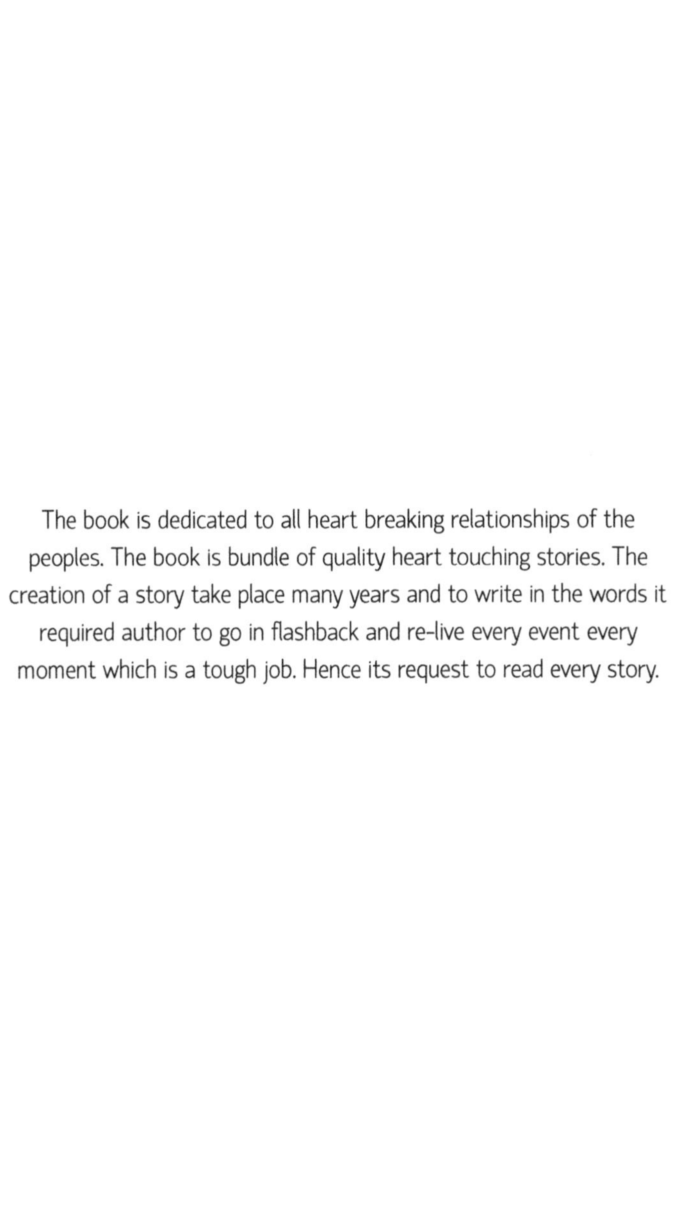

The book is dedicated to all heart breaking relationships of the peoples. The book is bundle of quality heart touching stories. The creation of a story take place many years and to write in the words it required author to go in flashback and re-live every event every moment which is a tough job. Hence its request to read every story.

Contents

Preface

The book has interesting stories which are woven in a manner which definitely binds the readers. Also embedding the science part will fascinate the readers in between the stories. The book depicts stories which are breaking of love bonds due to mis-conception and mis-understanding. It's a really pathetic situation when we have fast communication but we are losing interpersonal communication. We are having dry means of communication which don't have emotions but have emojis. Once you try to overcome this virtual world then only you can feel true nature's love for yourself.

About Author/s:

Mr. Sachin C Narwadiya

Mr. Sachin C Narwadiya written and published many books and some important one are Tear Drop A Love Story(English), Sainik Aur Swasthya(Hindi), Vo Saat

Saal(Hindi), Vigyan Yatra(Hindi), MCQs of Biochemistry(English), Let's enjoy Biochemistry Learning (English), My Journey in Science Communication(English). He is an author, poet and also a scientist. He has 20+ years of experience in Research Development writing and publishing.

Ms. Ankita Baheti

Ms. Ankita Baheti, is Electronics and communication engineer by profession from Rajasthan, currently settled in Qatar (after marriage). She had worked as Assistant Professor in Engineering college, Udaipur. She had always inclination towards arts and literature since childhood days. She is a bilingual writer, editor and reviewer, associated with many national and international literary groups where she gets accolades and acknowledgment for her poetries, articles, reviews, and stories. Her work is published in many recognized e-magazines, e-papers and is published co-author of 15+ anthologies; few prominent among them are "Women we know, Audacity of blank pages, Psithurism, Inquest: Ambers of life,

Metaphorphosis (international)". This is her first storybook along with Mr. Sachin Narwardia, where she will unfurl her story writing skill to the masses.

CHAPTER ONE

Triangle

That day when after a long time those friends met at a function, they were so happy that they forgot the pain of the longer duration of being apart. But when they met and organized a party in the car, which they usually did many times in the past, a wrong communication happened which ruined all of their friendship and trust forever. It is well said that in the roots of every dispute there will be either a girl or money (exceptions are there). After drinking and eating tasty foods in the car every one i.e Jaitavya, Shirish, Vipul, Rizul and Jagan felt too much enjoyment. The reason behind holding car parties is that the bars are too costly in Delhi-NCR and such frequent parties can not be sustainable to pocket. Alcohol is acting as a remedy to speak the thoughts and talks which one can't express while without it. Now Jaitevya started, "Dear Shirish, I heard from one of my common colleagues that a girl in the office who is too pretty and her name is Varonika, I feel both of you have a crush on each other." These words kept everyone in a piece of silence for a while. Shirish replied, "See I already have a girlfriend and I will have no crush on anybody other than my girlfriend". The discussion came to end with this clarification. But, Jaitavya expressed that he is having a crush on Veronika. Now the breaking of the bonding between friends started with these short conversations. Actually every one needed to trust each other and inside the car whatever was said during the party needed to be forgotten at the same time. But we forget good things and conversations and always remember the bad ones. The discussion was over on that day, but very next day Shirish called to Jaitavya and he expressed his grief over the phone that some body ruined his dignity by adding his name with Veronica. Jaitavya tries his best to convince Shirish but he is not able to listen and repeat the same thing. Finally it's the day when two friends and their friendship start breaking down due to a girl.

Let's start with some introductions of the story characters. These friends' names are Jaitavya, Shirish, Vipul, Rizul, Jagan and Devesh. All these friends worked in the same office and during corona time when offices were closed or opened with low capacities, they managed to meet and sit together, chit chat together, and occasionally drink alcohol together. The amazing fact was only one of them i.e Devesh got an infection of corona. Whole period of 1-2 years passed in full enjoyment and party timings. They made a whatsapp group too for deciding on parties and chatting there. Jaitavya is on the highest post among all of them and a little more senior, Shirish was a newcomer and the youngest in the group and also a good cricket player too. Vipul is from regions of mountains and he is always happy and has a smiling personality. Rizul, Jagan and Devesh are introverted and shy.

The story begins in 2019 when Shirish newly joins the office where all party boys are already there. Everyone after working the whole day for 5 days wishes to meet and greet over an alcohol party on Friday evening. All my friends were eagerly waiting for the day while on work and then that 2-3 hours of happy chatting in the party. The story is of Noida Sector 62 and after the party sometimes all went to B block market of sector 62 to have to eat tasty yummy momos.

When Shirish and Jaitavya were in the Delhi office then they used to taste mutton famous at Matka Peer Dargah and Khanna market while chicken shawarma at the concept restaurant of Lajpat nagar. The days were filled with joy of beer cane in the car with music and masti. Jaitavya used to guide Shirish to apply for the permanent jobs as he was on project, also they talked about past Girlfriends and their experiences. The days were filled with happier moments. In between Shirish also invited Jaitavya to his home also Jaitavya invited him too hence they became family friends. After 2 years at the start of 2021 the Vipul left job to join an NGO hence the backbone of the party organization has left us. Everyone felt sad but nothing can be done. The Jaitavya and Shirish got transferred to the Delhi office and then they became best friends. The reason behind it was their homes are in the same direction so they could share a car and went home together for initial 6 months. Jaitavya has a Maruti Wagon R-hybrid fuel model. The car is equipped with a touch screen android player and soothing music emitting speakers. Shirish has capabilities to drive with drink(not allowed as per prevailing laws) but in Delhi when you are stuck in a traffic Jam for hours nothing can be done except take a little drink and drive.

The days are passing and one day Shirish requested Jaitavya to guide his girl friend named Bhagyashree because Jaitavya is a poet, writer, and also a scientist. He can deliver the philosophy talk and after 2 pegs the talk was so impactful that the listener will forget all the world and drown in the words of Jaitavya. The request was well accepted by Jaitavya and an online talk organized over whatsapp video call. The talk started and Jaitavya said to Bhagyashree, "Welcome, hope you are fine and happy. I will explain some life changing thoughts with you in the next 5-10 min so be concentrate and listen. See dear there is God, and we all have the sign of God in ours as Soul. Whatever we do, we think, we speak, we give something to nature and as power law in science to every action there is equal and opposite reaction hence whatever you give will return to you same by the God. For example if you are in pain remembering God then God will increase your pain because God doesn't know our communicating language but he knows only the emotions we are sending to him. If you survey for the past 200 years you can find that those are richer and happy like landlords, kings are rich today also(about 80% of them are richer today) the reason is that they worship God in a happy and satisfied mood instead of any sorrow hence God increased and gave the same in return. The method of worship is also different in every religion. The best practiced method is of Muslims who always trust that Allah Pak is a light and worship directly to almighty God. The Hindu trust that the Hindu Dharma started from Om with light behind, hence it is called supreme soul, but to make people concentrate Hindus developed many idols of God and started worshiping them which is an indirect communication to God. Jesus also never claimed that he is God but he always explained that he is the son of God and God is actually a light. So, if we see all these religions have the same concept and same ideology. So if you start worshiping the real God directly in a happy mood you will get whatever you wish in life."

Bhagyashree was impressed with the conversation and felt happy. Thus days are passing and slowly Jaitavya is developing a one way liking and crush to Veronica which is also in the Delhi office. All of them eat together and as Veronica and Shirish like eating non-veg foods and Jaitavya is a good cook for Non-Veg foods he used to cook mutton and chicken for them and brought office for them. The tradition of eating so well planned that it used to happen once or twice a week. There is a big forest behind the Delhi office so after eating everyone started to walk to the Jungle cand chit chat about many things. Actually, this type of get together is needed in the time where everyone used to spend maximum time over screen. Screen viewing of mobile/computer disconnects you from nature from health.

After the incident the relations are becoming more and more dry. The party boys are becoming more away from each other. Shirish did his long pending engagement with another girl than his girlfriend(due to cast issue he was not able to marry Bhagyashree). He did not invite Jaitavya in his engagement but he invited Devesh,Rizul and Veronica. The missed understanding ruined a good friendship forever. Hence whatever we say in future we need to think twice before delivering words.

Sachin Narwadiya
Ghaziabad

Credit: https://pixabay.com/

CHAPTER TWO

Online Friendship

Sheetal was watering her plants. Suddenly, it started raining. Monsoon-the season of love. Yes! She calls the monsoon season of love, the reason behind it is, she feels it's the love of sky, which clouds bring with them. When it rains, sky pours love to earth and enriches earth's natural resources with love and life. Everything becomes so mesmerizing, magical and enticing. That petrichor fills the heart and mind with serenity and calmness. It's the best season, the season of life, the season of gratitude, the season of natural beauty. That's why Sheetal loves monsoon.

Sheetal, is a mother of two children, a boy and a girl, both well educated, settled in their lives, busy making their career and family. They are in different cities connected to parents over phone calls, video calls and sometimes visiting them as per time from their busy schedule or their requirements or just for the sake of break from their tiring life.

Sheetal was happily married or may be, could say she pretend to be happy in her marriage in all these years, just for the sake of society, parents esteem and children future. These all are pressure points build up by the so called society torch bearers. Everything was going smooth with the usual ups and downs faced by any family. But was she really happy, sometimes she use to think about it? But whenever she tried to share, it was always one or the other person, straight away shun her conversation saying that marriage means sacrifice. The synonym for marriage is adjustment. She always wonder why? Why only she has to adjust or sacrifice her dreams, her longings? Why can't her husband do that? Why this so called society is patriarchal? Why can't she freely say what she feels? Why she has to take the responsibility of being conventional parent?

But all these questions were answered. Gradually she started to accept the fact most of the women of our modern yet narrow minded society do. She was lost her individuality and started pretending to be one perfect happy family. She didn't realized when her smile, her behavior, her conversations became mechanical. She forget the last time she took the decision by herself. She like typical mother, engaged her whole life around her kids. Children grew up, took their decision for college, to job, to career, to choosing spouse. She was their to arrange everything whatever they wanted and however they wanted. Even the children forget that mother too is individual, she too have dreams, she too has her choice. But alas, everyone was happy so she happily did all the rituals or formalities which were required with time.

When children got busy in their own life, that was the time she got alone. That loneliness sometimes even beought depression but her sister use to say "its normal, phase, will pass by, don't over think about it." That time, lot and lot of alone time, brought her to social media. She began to find her old school, college friends. Chatting with them, brought a little confidence back. Remembering those golden days, she use to cherish the memoirs. By that time her husband 'Raj' also got retired, she thought, may be now they will spend time together and once again she will give afresh start to the relationship. May be now she could express herself to him and may now he will understand her and will encourage her to do what she wanted years back. She wanted to make a beautiful garden, she wanted to plant many trees, plants, herbs, shrubs. She wanted to place a swing in the garden, where could sit and enjoy the evening tea while looking the sunset. She could relish the sunrise, listening the chirping of birds, fragrance of flowers and the breeze. All these years, she always wanted it, but she never told to her husband, because according to him maintaining garden was tough job and also he didn't have time to soend that quality time with his wife. So he said no and sheetal simply agreed, because there was no other choice. But now, she will tell him about her wish and the idea how she wanted it to be made.

Sheetal's husband Raj was a businessman so even after retirement he was not really retired. For him, his work was always his first priority, then kids, then parents and then sheetal. She was always the last. Raj has never really cared about Sheetal's likes dislikes, her dreams, anything!

So Raj made himself busy with his friends, newspaper, consultancy, gossips. He made sure he would go out everyday for one or the other things like grocery, social work, playing, temples or just roaming. He didn't have time for Sheetal even after retirement. One day Sheetal told she wanted to do gardening and in front of their house, they have space so she can make good use of it, but her husband denied the idea. He said "instead you do it at the terrace, it's a lot more space and nobody will disturb you or will stop you from doing what you wanted to do." He didn't want any mess in the front entrance so very conveniently he asked

Sheetal to make a terrace garden.

One fine day, while surfing on social media, she joined a "terrace garden". It was a group for like minded people, who use to share their experience and learn about planting or get gardening tips. Sheetal always loved plants, gardening and taking care of different indoor and outdoor plants, so joined it without fail.

There, she accidentally met Sudheer. Sudheer was a retired professor, whose only daughter was settled in her life and his wife passed away three years back. He loved his wife, after losing him, he went to depression. But his daughter, took charge of everything and made her father bounce back from that hard time. Daughters are like that, they never leave you alone, one or the other way, they are comnected to you. Sudheer's daughter askwd her father to live with them. But Sudheer said "he want to live with her mother's memories which are there in their home and promise that he will engage himself in activities and would not go back to depression mode. If ever he will low, he will come to her or will call her home." As promised his daughter, he started his long lost hobby of gardening. He remembered he and his wife use to put plants in the smallest space they would get in their different homes. Finally when thwy bought their own home, both planted indoor plants and outdoor plantation wasn't possible due to shortage of space. After joining group he liked the idea of terrace gardening. He began putting his favorite plants there.

Sheetal and Sudheer were in separate cities, miles apart but surprisingly got hitched with a great connection. Initially it was merely about, gardening. But slowly they shared everything from their personal life to professional to worldly matters like from family to children to local markets, maids bitching, neighbours stories, country's best and worst, almost everything. She was alone from all these years. She was alone even after her husband's retirement but now she got someone who was there, who was there to listen her stories, who was there to laugh at her jokes, who was there to improvise her, whi was there to give her gardening ideas, who was there to encourage her, who was there to comment on her looks, who was there to even tease her by her crush's name, who was there to lend her shoulder while she cried over her past or her present ignorance of her husband. Sudheer also got someone who was there to tell him new food recipes, who was there to help in advising him in house core work, who was there to complain about him to his daughter if he forget the medicines, whi was there to smile, laugh, scold him and give him groceries tips. Sudheer's daughter was happy that atleast her father has got duch a good friend who take care of him even though never met him.

Sheetal started reliving her dreams after she came in contact with sudheer. Or she could say she actually started living after she began conversation with Sudheer. Before that she was existing what she did was for her children or husband or parents or their fake society's norms. But now, she was happy, she was joyous, she was more of herself.. She use to hum her favorite song while cooking, get ready in evening and usevto have her tea at her terrace garden swing. She started getting compliments from her neighbors as well. She started going for groceries and asked Raj that he take care of other things. Raj still unnoticed the changes Sheetal were having.

She use to be cheerful, positive, grateful all the time. She started socializing. She herself noticed that change. Unlike Raj, people around her also noticed that changed. They started gossiping about her. This society and people around us have this work only, if someone's happy, they make them feel bad about it, depress them or question the integrity or authenticity, and id someone is sad or in grief, they are happy, yet gossip about it.

So soon Sheetal's happiness was not likes by many people and they started saying " At this age Sheetal has affair, she is not good, she should not do such things, she should think of her children, what impact will they have in their life, everything she had, still she was sad but now how happy she is, Raj is so innocent, he trust his wife blindly...etc" People started to sympathise with Raj. Raj got this gossip into his ears. Initially he ignored but soon he noticed the changes in Sheetal and he was worried. He was worried that Sheetal is happy without him. He was angry and in that he called Sheetal's sister 'Uma' and told her everything, his point of view, his part, people gossips and worries of future of children.

Soon Uma, came to Sheetal's house to meet her. Sheetal was her see her elder sister. She was chirping like a bird. Uma was surprised by her behavior. Sheetal had lot of things to tell her, she waa confused where to start from. Before she could aay anything Uma asked her "what's going on? Who's sudheer? Why u talk about him and talk to him so much?"

"Have you lost it? What Raj will do when he will come to know about Sudheer? How will he react? How children will take this? In few years you will be grandmother, all this things, doesn't look good on you. Wake up Sheetal, wake up, its high time, what are you doing qith your life? What do you think of yourself? We are not stars who can have such controversies in life. Stop Sheetal, before it gets too late.."

Sheetal got up and said "Uma Di, jdid you looked my terrace garden? Come i will show you, its so beautiful and soothing. Come have a look" and she holded Uma's hand to take her to terrace.

Uma was puzzled, she removed her hand and holded her and said " did you listen to what I just said? Or you have became deaf? Or you do not want to listen and understand? Understand.ny sister, we all love you, we don't want your name to get indulge in such bad gossip. You have a reputation, we have a reputation, which should be strain free in any condition, Sheetal, i hope you understand, what i trying to say."

Sheetal smiled and said "ofcourse Uma Di, i understand. I understand perfectly amd completely what all you want to say and what all of you want to do. But di do you understand me?

It's been years, i am married to raj, u never asked, why did i turn silent, where am i lost, where is my confidence and why am i carrying a fake smile? But now, when i am living not merely existing, i am problem to everyone. Everyone, my neighbors to society people to servants of this house to you, everyone, is staring at me with a big question mark, as if i have committed a crime or a murder.

Now when i am laughing my heart out u r asking? Now when i am beautiful inside out, you are questioning.

Raj, who did not had time through his whole working life, who does not have time for me now, is suddenly putting this allegations. Did you asked him, before questioning me, that why Sheetal turned so? Why you are not the reason for her happiness. Infact, Raj, you should be the one, atleast after retirement. But no, you straight away cane to me and started bombarding questions one after other."

"What answers you want to listen tell me that first. Infact why you need answers now? When you all were not ready yo listen to me years back, how stupid of me to expect that you will listen to me now. You didn't understand then, you will not understand now. Rather than misunderstanding me, you should have have thought something good about me, for the sake of our relation and bond we share. Raj misunderstood me, i am ok with that, society, society don't understand people, they simply judge. But I don't take their judgement seriously anymore. I spoiled my whole life because of this. I would have been something else, rather than just being a simple housewife, but you all killed my dreams and dismissed my decisions. And now at this point of time you are reminding of my duties and responsibilities.

I have done all my duties and responsibilities with full devotion. But now i want to live for myself.

Hence, stop building unnecessary pressure on me again? I know what am i doing... "

Her sister said but "you can't rely on such online friend, how can you trust someone? You haven't met that person! May be he can be cheater, this can be a trap or he could be fraudster, he can harm our reputation, he can ransome, he may blackmail you or....'

Before she could complete her statement, Sheetal interrupted and said "not every online friend needs to be looked upon suspiciously. Some people are genuine too, the world us not a dark place to live in. And trust, it's built over generosity with time. You know me since childhood, still you don't have trust on me, so might not trust anyone. But i have trusted an individual, who is a hood friend of mine, who has always supported me, who is happy when i am happy, who is sad when i am sad and try to cheer me out, who loves his wife, who has a wonderful daughter, whi has family which trust him, rather that putting him in family court and who do not disect his feelings, rather who respect him, his friend and look at the relationship in a healthy manner."

"Tell me, if it had been Raj, and i was suspicious, what you would have have suggested me?"

I tell you, you would have sai " they are just friends, what's a big deal, Sheetal have faith on Raj" but when i have a friend with whom i can share, i can laugh, i can fulfill my old hobby, or i can simply say i can be myself, you have so many questions! Aren't you happy, that finally after years your sister is so cheerful?

So i beg you, please stop judging me and let me live peacefully."

All that she said in a one go and left for the terrace garden. Suddenly the phone rang and screen flashed Sudheer's name. She was humming her favorite song and there was no guilt on her face, she confidentiality, merrily went to her terrace garden to pour love to her plants and picked up the call !

That online friendship has helped Sheetal to be beautiful inside out, without pretending to be someone else anymore! Its mere people's missed understanding that let individual suffer. Sometimes the suffering is too lengthy and it you are do habitual to it, that it take time to understand that society is for our betterment not judgement.

And not always when man and woman share close relationship its love, it can be PURE, BEAUTIFUL, SERENE FRIENDSHIP.

Ankita Baheti

Credit: https://pixabay.com/

CHAPTER THREE

Shower of love

Credit: https://pixabay.com/

It is a story of a Love and the breaking of love for life time. The end is emotionally sensitive and learning also. I usually start with the end of story and then in flashback the story is running, this style leads the readers to more connection and interest for the story. So not further delay I start narrating a story. It's a story of an Extramarital affair which our Indian society does not accept at all.

The bell of a mobile phone is ringing. Alok received the call and just moved out of home because the call is from his girlfriend Sneha at Pune and he is in Delhi. She said to him, "Dear, last time before 1 week you came to Pune and we met and to inform you that I am so tensed because

I got pregnant." The information is very shocking to Alok because he is already married and having kids too. She also inform him that you come come back to Pune and please do needful to abort it as I am unmarried and can't keep it." Alok who recently came back from an office tour made that mistake and without safety made a relationship with Sneha. Now his pocket and time are not permitting him to go again. So he replied silently in a peaceful voice, " See, I can not come again but I have many Doctor friends, Pharmacists also I will make available to you the Medical Termination of Pregnancy kit-MTP kit and it will help you to get rid of this problem." But all in vain and she cut the call with a promise not to keep any further contact. The moment was so troublesome for both of them.

The story started 5 years ago in a present miserable condition. When Alok was in Pune and alongwith his job doing part time teaching in a college too. He met Sneha, a receptionist there. Sneha is a shy Girl, being in her 38 years of age she is not married. She has her sisters also not married and father is retired. So she slowly came closer with Alok and they together started visiting other offices for official purposes. One day Alok informed her that there is one good resort there and we can go roam and come back, so they planned to visit on Saturday, as Saturday is Alok's holiday. So, he picked her up on his bike and they went to the Resort. There many couples are visiting and they take room for love making. Now inside the room Alok intended for a romance and relationship with her, then she denied and not accepted the same. Alok had the principle that without the acceptance of a girl he never made any relations. So finally they checked out of the room and came back. On the way Alok didn't talk much and remained silent as he was too annoyed with her. Sneha after 1-2 days realized that she made a mistake that broke the heart of Alok, so she broke out ice and started from herself. She not only admitted her mistake but also gave her acceptance for the next meet. The next meet was decided and time came soon. Alok was very happy to have his love in reality in his arms. They went to a costly hotel as both have to keep everything confidential. During the relationship Alok observed an amazing thing that Sneha never removed the blanket from her and Alok during all the time of love making so that not the air of the hotel can touch her body, also she is frightened about hidden cameras in the hotel. The Alok has the best experience with her or one can say its life time experience. Because it is general tendency that after orgosome there is no further sex between a girl and boy but in this case it was not there and after ejaculation Alok used to do 30-40 minutes round of sex with her. There he found something new, something extra in her as her skin color became darker during love making. Alok's and Sneha eating habits also matched and they both like non-veg dishes. So the scene of meeting and love making did not remain for further as Alok got selected in another company in Jaipur and he left Pune at last. Sneha was so sad but she couldn't do much.

Now whenever time permits Alok used to come to Pune and they met. But the situation never remained the same and the situation always changed. The situation changed with one wrong step taken by Alok and after that breaking of a good love started with grief and sad moments. The story is not at par with society norms which advocate marriage and disregard extramarital affairs but every marriage is not successful. Hence there is always exploration of new relations by married men and women. The society needs a revisit to the structure and an in depth study of each country's marriages and live in relations for a less stressful future in life. Finally the Sneha disconnected from Alok and they got grief for their whole life.

Sachin Narwadiya

Ghaziabad

CHAPTER FOUR

Love like wine -Red or White

Credit: https://pixabay.com/

People come and go out of our life. They play their roles and when the role vanishes they leave silently that we can not know when and what happened. Life is like this only those who are with us today are not confirmed for tomorrow but somebody will be there as human beings are social animals. The story is interesting and full of something new which readers wish to read. So let's start a new story.

It is a story of two best friends Jatin and Subrato. Both did their education together in M.Sc. Jatin became a scientist while Subrato became an Army officer. They used to meet in their native place Lucknow. As Jatin used to visit to cancer hospital and medical college as visiting lecturer he came in contact with a Doctor, Dr. Sonal Bankar.

The Dr. Sonal was a girl who is unpredictable, beautiful, open minded. She had lots of qualities and intelligence in her. The Jatin after recent breakup ususally felt alone and as we know lonliness is the enemy of mankind. After M.Sc Jatin and Subrato became connected via phone only and both has same problem of lonliness. The same feeling is there in Dr. Sonal. The Dr.Sonal and Jatin bacame friends after some days of meeting. Dr.Sonal is look like a famous heroin Rani Mukharjee. She ususally wear glasses which enehnaces her beauty. The new freindship always attract each other to know more about each other hence massages and conversation is on peak between Jatin and Sonal. Slowly Jatin felt that he alone can not handle the Sonal because she was too demanding for time. So Jating introduced Subroto to her and let them talk over phone too. The Jatin used to chat and connected with Sonal during day time as he was in office while Subroto being posted in Jammu and Kashmir in Army connect with her during night. Now whatever Subroto and Sonal chats or communicated the same was discussed in between Jatin and Subroto. So Subroto and Jatin being best friends know always what the Sonal wishes from both. Slowly Jatin felt that Subroto involved emotionally with Sonal and during chat in night proposed her which she accepted. Subroto cried too in night when both talk on phone with each other. Jatin also feeling love for Sonal which she too feeling. Sonal's inclination is more towards Jatin due to same field of working, Jatin is as Scientist more knowledged than Subroto, also Jatin is in same city of Sonal so meeting is not far away. Now Jatin and Sonal started meeting weekly in restaurents for tea and snacks and sometimes drinks too. Jatin cleared his intrest of making love and sex with Sonal to his intrests she did not deny or accept.

One fine morning when Jatin was busy in preparing for his office he got call from Sonal to come to his home. Jatin understood what was not spoken from Sonal and after ready for office took bike and went to Sonal home. She told that she is alone but up floor her aunty is there. Jatin and Sonal started talks and discussion. Slowly she started smooching Jatin because Jatin was afraid of having Aunty in home. Slowly Jatin too involved but excietment was on its peak. Both have first time relationsship on that day. After that Jatin went to office and he was too tired of sex and excitemnt. As Jatin used to share with Subroto about Sonal he told him with excietment. Subroto also now felt to meet her. He took long leave from his job and came to the native city where both Jatin and Sonal were there. That was first time all three met in a mall and lively discussion held between them. Jatin went away to home because his wife is calling for soem work, but Subroto took Sonal in his car for long drive. They had fun in car but not complete relationship as Sonal denied to make with him. But promised for future meeting with Subroto. The Subroto used to meet Sonal when he was in City and they both drinked wine/whisky as token of enjoyment.

After completion of leave Subroto started preparation for his return and he had to stay in Delhi for 1-2 days as transit stay. He after reaching Delhi told Sonal to come Delhi in morning and leave in night by flight to his proposal she accepted and Subroto made her tickets. Jatin was aware of this but he did not reacted as Subroto being his friend he wished that his friend need some enjoyemnt and relaxation. He was of openion that serving an army personnel is like serving country indirectly

Now as per plan the meeting completed successfully between Subroto and Sonal but the enjoyment with Sonal recieved by Jatin with expenses for that Subroto spends money on flight and hotel.

After return from Delhi, Sonal and Jatin started quarrel slowly for some useless topics. The level of quarrel reached to giving of vulgure comments and gali(bad words) in sms and talks. But when time passed slowly they both felt thier mistakes and settle issues between them. The time was tensed time for both of them. After settlement they both met and drank wine enjoyed. That day Sonal who was very money savy gave an exciting offer of party to Jatin with his 3 frinds Nikhil, Shilpa and Umesh.

Jatin was happy to accept that and he managed to convience his friends for alcohol party in family bar. It was a good time for Jatin as his wife also went to her parents home with kids. The Jatin got ready in evening with his bet outfits and fragrance of deo. All of them met in family bar 10 kms away from Jatin home and started enjoying drinks over lots of live discussions. Sonal paid extra attention over Jatin and let him drink some more pegs than his capacity. Still Jatin drunk with eyes of her and didnot know he was drunk too much untill feeling of vomitting after 2-3 hours. He just step out from table and went to bathroom and vomitted. He felt littile better and meanwhile he came back party was over Sonal paid bill and they stood up to go downstairs. Sonal in parking after all left huged to Jatin and then she started her two wheeler for home and left. Now its really challanging job for Jatin to drive his bike to home after such huge drinking of alcohol. But he managed and with more caution he drived bike reached home and when he get in bed he go sleep. The good times never remains forever and that happened with this fine story. Slowly Sonal stopped talks with both and then she got married in Mumbai to a fellow of Prayagraj. She was in touch for more few years over phone and slowly got disconnected. Subroto and Jatin are friends and meet occasionally but remeber her as true friend of both of them. Who told love happened with one person only thats not love thats possessiveness. The love of Sun shines everyone equally, the love of Earth spreads equally on each and every living animals plants so stop love for one only. Such thinking will drown all society in deep into grief.

Sachin C Narwadiya

Ghaziabad

CHAPTER FIVE

My bestie

Credit: https://pixabay.com/

"She had always been my friend from the day one i entered my school. Yes, right from nursery till i left my school after 12th. But that last day of our boards exams would turn into last day of our friendship, i never thought that.." said Krisha, to her doctor Dr. Nishika.

Krisha was an introvert girl. She didn't had many friends throughout her school days and even in college. She was an emotional and truly loyal person. But she had gone through out of emotional stuff and had a heavy baggage, which she was not able to deal after certain period of time. She went into depression on the stage where she was supposed to be more confident and her life had just started by then. She just completed her college and started a job. She was happy with her smooth and simple life but then something happened which triggered lot of anxiety and past experiences from her life also shaked her. She was unable to decide, she is doing right or wrong. She was that person, who use to take stand for any wrong or against law, when she was in college. But that incident shattered her badly and she started doubting herself. She used to look at nothing for hours. Sometimes use to cry. Sometimes just doing nothing and laying down.

That's when her parents took help of Dr. Nishika, who is a good psychiatrist of the city. Initially they thought it's just a phase and they could deal with it. But soon they realized they need a professional help. So they started her sessions with doctor.

Krisha when first met Dr. Nishika, she was clumsy, terribly confused, completely shattered and underconfident. Then her sessions started, slowly she started to talk about her life, her likes, dislikes. Today Krisha told doctor about her childhood friend Priti. She was her best friend. When they started school, the teacher made them sit together and Krisha got her first friend Priti. Slowly they became good friends and then best friends. They use to share everything to each other. Both their families knew about their friendship and they use to take care of both the girls. Even after school, they use to go to each others home to play, or cycling or roaming around. They use to play pranks on their classmates. They were popular in school.

The time passed and they were in class 9. All the other students sometimes use to get jealous of their friendship.

Once an article vame in newspaper about friendship that two peopke were friends for 17 years. Priti looked at it and said to Krisha "we will break the record and our friendship will be forever, timeless, till the last breathe."

It was not that Krisha and Priti never fought, even they use to fight but soon use to resolve the matter. It was never long than a day that they haven't talked to each other. Teachers also sometimes use to complain to Krisha's parents that Krisha talks too much in class to Priti. Once when they were in class 4, it was decided to make them sit separate. But within 7 days Krisha's health started detoriating and her parents requested teacher to make them sit together. Teacher agreed and said to Krisha "no too much talking" Krisha smiled and said "ok ma'am"

Krisha was the topper in class and Priti was an average student. But it never came in between thir friendship, neither their parents bothered about it. They were happily sailing in their life boats with full boost of friendship fuel. But what fate holds ahead is never know to us.

One day Krisha's Grandfather passed away. Krisha was very much attached to him. She was broken. She use to cry a lot. When Priti came to know about it, she stood by her and made her understand that she has to accept the reality. It took her 6 months to come over it. Then she returned to normal routine. But she use to miss her grandfather very much. For her, getting emotionally detached was the biggest and toughest task.

One day principal called Priti and told that her father met an accident and he is in hospital. She said "Do not worry, we all are with you. You go to hospital and your things will be sent to home". She was in such situation that she just left for hospital and told no one about it. Soon the news broke to whole class and Krisha also came to know.

After school she told her mom that she going to hospital to meet Priti, she might need help. Her mother said ok and asked her if Priti needs any help, tell her, they will arrange. Krisha went to hospital, in fact all the classmates came to meet Priti and her father. Krisha holded Priti's hand and said "everything will be fine. Believe me. Just stay strong and if you need anything let me know." As soon as she saw her father in hospital bed, she remembered her grandfather whom she lost six months back and negative thoughts came to her mind.

So Krisha decided to leave the hospital and came home. Before coming she said to Priti that if she needs any sort of help, do not hesitate, just call her. Krisha's parents also went next day and met Priti's parents. Priti's father operation was successful and he was out of danger.

But Priti felt that Krisha should have stayed there with her instead of leaving. And Krisha after coming home constantly prayered for Priti's father good health but she was unable to hold the sight of that hospital bed and patients. She wanted Priti's father get back home soon and nothing wrong happens to him. As she came to know uncle is fine she ran to temple and thanked god for listening to her prayers.

But after this incident slowly and slowly a rift came in Krisha and Priti's friendship. Priti being an introvert girl didn't have many friends, in school, only few selective friends. But Priti had other friends too, so slowly she started avoiding Krisha. Krisha felt bad but thought may be she needs her space. She even tried to ask Priti that is there something she felt Krisha did wrong? But Priti simply said "no, you are over thinking. We are friends and nothing i felt bad. You just take care."

After their 10th boards Krisha took science stream and Priti opted commerce, so they were busy in their own world. But they use to meet in school, talk and motivate each other at times. Time flew and now was the time when they had their boards.

While they were in 12th, it was their last in school, new friends, new subjects and new life awaiting after school for them. Their was a common subject both chose was "Hindi". Priti was always good in that while Krisha use to study hard for it. It was their last board exam and Krisha called Priti to ask her that can she come to her home, to clear some doubts? But Priti clearly said NO and cut the call. Krisha was surprised and didn't said anything. Next day when they met, Priti came causally to Krisha and said "hey hi". But today Krisha didn't replied, as she was angry. She thought ok, she said no, but atleast she could have helped her over phone on the topic. (That time google and internet was not that common and was not used by everyone. There were only landline phones at home)

But after that Priti never called Krisha, never came to her home, never talked afterwards. Krisha use to wonder, why, why Priti turned so? What wrong i did? Why Priti broke their so long friendship? With time she realized that whenever they use to fight, it was always Krisha who use to talk first, Priti never did. But that doesn't mean that Priti was always right.

Krisha came in pharmacy college, she got new friends. She use to meet her other classmates from school who now turned to be her good friends. In college, Krisha was no longer an introvert, with time she got confidence and she use to take part in all other activities too. She was topper in college too and popular in college. She was straight forward in her views but still she had few friends only. She was always like that. But in final year of college she had a fight with her close friend Riya and rest is repeated history. But the impact was not that strong, as it was at the time of Priti. She still use to sometime ask God that why Priti did that and now Riya. Is she the real problem? Is she wrong in her opinion? Are other people correct? Why she has to loose her part along with each friend she looses? There were no answers, but somehow she would reach to conclusion and move ahead in life.

After college, she got a job in pharma company and she was happy to be the part of it. Soon her parents started searching match for Krisha so that she gets married and settle down.

One day, they found the boy and his family to be appropriate for their daughter. Vishu, the boy was working in am MNC in finance department and his parents were their friend's friend. So they decided, let first children meet each other and then they would decide further.

On decided date, Krisha met Vishu and felt he is the one, she want to spent rest of her life. So after coming home she said yes, to her parents for Vishu. Krisha's parents called Vishu's parents and told their decision. Vishu's parents were happy, they said wven they like Kriaha and want to make her the part of their family. She got engaged to Vishu.

But then started the real drama. Vishu started mentally torturing her over phone calls, sometimes demanding something, sometimes just scolding her for nothing, sometimes abusing Krisha's parents for no reason. She slowly and slowly was suffocating in that relation. The courtship pwriod, which the most beautiful time for any couple, had become a burden to her. But she loved her parents and so for their name & reputation in the society, she was tolerating all the rubbish and mess Vishu was creating. Alas, in the end, ahe started to choke out but still.maintaimes a dignified silence in front of her parents so that they are happy.

The marriage day was fixed and Vishu's drama increased day by day. She uses to cry a lot. She used to stay sad and unhappy. Her parents noticed that change and tried to talk to Vishu and parents. But all of them turned deaf ears. Thus, finally they took the decision to call off the marriage and broke the engagement.

The constant mental trauma by Vishu had made bad and strong impact on Krisha. She had self doubt, she used to ask her mom "is she so bad and dumb that she can't understand people? She can't choose good friends, How can she choose a life partner? She left her job and used to lock herself in room and cry.

After certain days her parents finally contacted doctor Nishika for help.

Doctor got to know her story from her perspective. But as Krisha use to speak about her past and all the incidents where she became emotionally vulnerable, doctor noted down the points and came to know about her problem. Its quite common in emotional attached people. They have to learn to use wisdom and make themselves emotionally steong rather than getting weak.

Initially even medications were given to her by doctor. But with time, medicines were stopped and she was given different exercises and sent to workshops. She even sent to a vacation.

She agreed to go to vacation to a historical place where she met Ajay. Ajay was enthusiastic, loving, joyful person. He was an IT professional. He also came for a vacation. Krisha and Ajay had common interests so they use to go together to see the places. Spending time with Ajay made

Krisha happy too. She felt light and cheerful. Before heading to their respective citirs back they exchanged phone numbers.

After coming back, from vacation, Krisha was truly refreshed and ready to face the world again. Her parents and doctor were happy with the progress.

Doctor said "Krisha misunderstanding happens, and due to which you sometimes loose a good friend, may be ur bestie but it doesn't mean you can't trust others and stop living. It's ok. May be Priti and Riya and even Vishu had some other priorities, but that doesn't mean you were at fault or you were wrong. You did what you could do. Rest is fine. You always be cheerful like this and do not doubt yourself. Sometimes its just misunderstandings to be blamed and nobody. So be happy and live your dreams"

Krisha started giving job interviews and she got one soon but in other city. She has to move to Mumbai for the job. Coincidentally Ajay was working in Mumbai. She asked him about the company, area, details and a home to search near to office.

Ajay was amazed and so happy, he said he will make all the arrangements and help her in every possible manner. She came to mumbai and shifted to a flat near to her office. Ajay helped as he said. She was happy, atleast she has a friend in this unknown city. On weekend's he use to take her to markets and places to get her friendly with the city. He started liking Krisha. He fall in love with her simplicity, her eyes, her long black curly hair, her smile. When he used to be with her and she would tell her about the office gossip, he was lost in her voice. Sometimes Krisha use to get angry, that you don't listen to what i say. In reply to that Ajay would say "you don't know when you speak and tell about your office i wonder, i would work there to see all this drama by myself" and both would laugh together. All he wanted was, to keep Krisha happy. Soon he realized he loves her and want her in his life forever but was afraid, that if she rejects him, he will loose a friend too.

But one day he decided that he will tell his feelings to her. That evening, sitting at beach, looking at the sunset Ajay proposed Krisha for marriage. All of a sudden, all that past moments came to her in a quick flashback moment but then she closed her eyes, remembered was doctor said and when she opened her eyes, she was smiling and said "ofcourse, yes, feeling is mutual. You are my bestie. Before my life partner, you are my Friend to whom i can share and trust. Love you my Bestie"

Life is full of surprises and ups & downs. What we need is to learn and move ahead. We can’t hold the burden of heavy baggage of past for long, it will hurt us only. As it’s always advised "travel light" ; it applies to the life journey too. Remember "travel light" and keep enjoying.

Ankita Baheti

Qatar

CHAPTER SIX

Brocken Marriage

Credit: https://pixabay.com/

One fine day the sun was shining bright, Supriya made a tweet. The teeet was watched by Soham and he saw the face of a beutiful lady Supriya. The Soham was working as Scientist in space science and had many years of experience of Research and Developement. He was aware that Supriya is also a Researcher in a reputed Institute. The tweet liking and comments intiatied a freindship thread among both of them. They called each other over phone as they are not in same city and spoken about career and educational aspects. Supriya is a pretty girl and doing work as anchor in Doordarshan. She is intelligent but weak in English which is a crieteria of Indians to judge other intelligence which is absolutely wrong but each and every one became victim of such judgemnts. The Supriya in her Research work is in need help of Soham and as Soham passion is research he agreed but on chargeable basis so that she will not feel that Soham has any other intentions. Slowly their talks begin and long phone calls started between them. They tried to know each other over calls and likes each others way of communication vibes. Soham started guiding her in a professional way. Supriya is 3 sisters only and she is eleder one the unfortunate part is all of in age of marriage but unmarried. They lost their father some years before so her mother and she with sisters become working force for earning money for getting bread and butter. Supriya had societal pressure for marriage some auncle took one proposal of Bihari guy for marriage. As Supriya family is simple they understood the Bihari guy is intelligent and doing PhD too they accepted the proposal and finally she got marriage. After marriage for some days she went to her husband home at Bihar. The girl with city living culture can not able to accept the backward type thinking of her husband and his mother. After 15 days she came back to home. The husband used to tocher her for sexual relationship and he had hydrocele disease too. Soham was not connected to her for few months as Supriya went under truamatic situations due to all torchers she got from husband and family. But as they all are only females at home she dont wish to give furthure trouble to her sisters and mothers she did not took any legal step in this regard.

After rteurn back to her home after some months she again called Soham she detailed everything she faced and being emotional person Soham also cried for her. Now Soham again started helping her but they are doing it secretly becsuase public thinks wrong always whenever a two persons male female became friends in India.

Now she focussed on her PhD and after that only she will file divorce case she decided. She finally got award of degree and completed her PhD. Now after that she filled a case for divorce which is a long battle to win. She did a fight becoming more storngder girl in society.

Sachin C Narwadiya

Ghaziabad

CHAPTER SEVEN

A story of multiples

Credit: https://pixabay.com/

One fine morning Rishi got a call for loan purpose. He is at his office as he works for a Multi- National Company. He recieved call from Vandana and she talks too politely. Both talked with each other and slowly their talks increased. Rishi is married person and he had kids too but he always in search of extra marrital affairs because his wife is not giving him satisfaction that he required. Rishi and Vandana now became friends and continued for talks. Vandana was a girl who previously worked as Teacher in village of Uttar Pradesh. She is intelligent but had sad story too. She left her husband after 4-5 years of marriage as she know that her husband was a Gay. Her husband relations was with a servant at home. She had 2 sons too of the husband previous wife who diad and as she has more sisters at home she accepted to marry with him. Slowly she earned from school as Teacher and made some property but when she did not get what she want from her husband she left him. When she came to Delhi she met with a nice gentelemen named Krishna. Krishna was also marriaed to a wrong witch type female and they lived together but Krishna and Vandana slowly started loving each other. In this story now there is entry of Rishi. Rishi and Vandana became friends and talks about each other life. The Vandana and Rishi scheduled their first meet and they meet near ametro station in Delhi. Both impressed from each other and their vibes concise for their next meet. The Rishi knows that what Vandana needs love with some freedom. So they started roaming sometimes outing too and slowly came closer. The nice part is that the Vandana home in Delhi is close to Rishi office say just 30 min distance. So whenever both feels to meet they schedule meeting and met eat drink coffee/tea. Sometimes Rishi used to help her financially also. Krishna wife when went away Krishna started to live in with Vandana and that made some distance between Vandana and Rishi. But both loved together hence they understood together and they used to meet but once in a month or 2-3 months also. But their love thier understanding is not thursty for the meeting.

The Wife of Krishna filed a divorce case in the village and fir that purpose Krishna had to visit the village often in 2-3 months. The frinedship of Vandana and Rishi is maturing with time and they cooporate each other by listening each others problems. The understanding between Vandana and Rishi missed when once they are in relationship using proper protection too after that some days later Vandana called and told she was pregnent. The news was too shocking for Rishi and he knows he used proper protection but it is well said that in debate you cant defeat a girl specially a girlfriend. So finally he took her Medical Termination of Pregnancy-MTP kit which resulted in the abortion at home. This all given lots of pain to her and that she had to keep secret from Krishna.

Slowly after few months the situation became normal as the best medicine in world is time which cure every hardship by the ointment of the forgable memories.

Sachin C Narwadiya

Ghaziabad

CHAPTER EIGHT

Half conversation

Credit: https://pixabay.com/

Ramya put the bucket under the tap and opened it. She was watching the water pouring into the bucket. The continuous dripping sound of water and the constant layer of it. She was watching it and forgot the time count. She was lost in the past memories in that moment. Bucket was filled and water started to flow out of bucket but she was unaware. She was so much lost that neither she could hear nor she could see what is going on.

Suddenly voice of Riti brought her back to present, she was screaming "mom, watch, water is flowing out, close the tap and you please be careful while coming out, its slippery"

Ramya said "sorry Riti, i just forgot to off the tap and all this happened"

Riti said " It s okay mom, you please take care of yourself and come slowly out.. its water all over the place so better be cautious"

Ramya slowly came out and then she said "let me clean it up". Riti stopped her saying "no, maid will come and she will do, till then i am opening the drain so the water sinks out"

Ramya was trying hard to pretend that she is alright and nothing to worry. But Ramya and Riti both knew that she is just faking it. Riti wanted to talk but she had such an hectic day that she didn't had the energy to speak and discuss. She thought they will have dinner and sleep. Morning first thing is she will talk to mom and will ask her what is she thinking about.

Quietly both had the dinner and Ramya said Mom i am too tired, i am going to bed, so you better take your medicine and sleep now. I will not sleep till you will not sleep and then i will have headache you know. So tell me what you want?" and giggled to make the situation normal. Ramya took medicine and went to bed. So Riti also went to sleep.

But Ramya, sleep was miles away from her eyes. She was just lyiy on the bed and once again went to the past memories.

It was a beautiful cloudy day. Ramya loved Clouds and Sun playing hide and seek. She came home from college, it was her final year. When she came home, she saw a new family sitting in her home and her parents are talking to them like known them for long. As she entered her mother said "that's our daughter Ramya, she is doing B.Sc. and this month end is her final exams". Ramya looked at her mother with questions in her eyes "why are you telling all this to these unknowns?" But she qas quiet as it was not the right place or situation to question. There was a boy sitting and staring at her continuously. She looked at him and raised an eyebrow asking "what?" To which he answered nothing by nodding his head and smiled. Both the parents asked Ramya and Adesh to go and show her their house. Ramya took Adesh for her home tour. She showed her all the rooms and then went to terrace and said "that's my favorite place" and Adesh looked at the beauty there was awestruck. He said " surely it is. It is an amazing place Ramya, i loved it. You made all these art pieces and paintings?" She said "no, not all, few." Rest was done by her father and grandmother. Now Adesh started telling about himself. He studied medical and for masters he went to America. He is planning to settle there. And asked her "does she want to go to America?" Ramya said "sure..." Listening that he was so happy that he just went to his parents to say "it's a YES". He didn't listened her whole sentence or waited for her and Ramya when she turned back she was puzzled that where Adesh is? She waited there then went downstairs and shocked to see that both the families were happy and joyful and greeting each other. She was confused. Meanwhile Adesh Mother came and said "we got out daughter in law, just as we wanted" and gave Ramya sweet to eat.

She didn't knew how to react or respond because she didn't had the least idea that it was her marriage proposal going on with the guy who is settled abroad. But she felt after they will leave she will talk to her parents.

As Adesh and his family left she said "mom dad i am not going to leave to alone here and go him to setlle abroad. Her father said "you said yes then he came and told everything. Ramya its very good family and boy is also nice. He will keep you like a queen. What else we want and you keep coming to us when you feel like meeting us or we will also come to meet you there. With this reason we can also visit America". Her mother was also so happy that God answered her prayer, their only daughter got such a good match.

So just after her exams, Ramya and Adesh got married and within a year he took her America with him. Ramya never had dreamt to go to abroad and settle there. She only wanted to visit new places and countries and come back to her home country. But Adesh listened her half conversation that day and result is she is here. Initially it was hard but slowly she adjusted with new people, situation, conditions.

But Adesh, he was busy with his studies and jo mb on weekdays and party with friends on weekends. It was okay to party once, twice but every week, Ramya was not happy with that. She tried to talk about this but Adesh would simply say you stay home if you want but i want to meet my friends and this so happening life here and you being boring, try to adjust or be here. Don't stop me ok."

Slowly as happens in marries life, their arguments increased, them fights and then always a statement from Adesh "go back to your parents and leave me,if you have so much problem then no need to stay here." Listening that she would cry amd Adesh male ego would satisfy and he thought he won and she has to agree to his terms and conditions.

Ramya was in pain but had no one to tell the truth. Because she knew her parents will not be able to handle this and anything negative cam happen, so she tolerated his mental torture. But slowly it converted to physical torture too.

One day she was vomiting all whole and feeling sick. He being a doctor didn't look after Ramya. She went to hospital and she got to know that she is pregnant. She didn't knew, she should be happy or sad with the news. When she told Adesh to her surprise he waa ao happy. He called everyone and told the news. From that day he took care of her pamper her. She was happy that atleat for child he is not that rude. If not a good husband, atleast he will be a good father. With that she thought she will also try to change her behavior towards Adesh. But in 7th month Adesh got to know that its a girl child, he wanted a son, so his behavior towards Ramya changed again. She was surprised that living in America he was so narrow minded. After Riti's birth, Adesh just didn't care about Ramya and Riti. He shifted to other city and told hee that once everything settles he will bring them. But that day didn't came. Initially he use to came once a month and would gave them money for their living. But slowly he started saying to Ramya that now Riti is 3years so you should start working and take care of yourself n your daughter. She shouted "what do you mean by your daughter? Is it only mine? Its not yours? What are you hiding? What do you want exactly?" Adesh said "divorce. I don't have feelings for you or Riti. Its better you start your life again and let me live my life my way"

Ramya didn't expected that. She was stunned. She said what will you tell parents? He said i fold my parents, you think how you will tell your parents and your drama, please i am sick of it."

She felt as if whole world has come to an end. She has lost her father last year and this news will take her mother too. So she decided not to tell anything to her mother. But soon her mother too left for heavenly abode. All this hussle went in her life but she was fighting.

She came to India for last rites of her mother. And decided that she will not go back America.

She started a job there in her home town. She had her parents home to live and Riti was 5years only but was mature then her age. She supported her mother in every possible manner. Time flied and Riti was now working in an MNC. She was software engineer. She got the offer to work on site in America. Once again this place came where Ramya had left her all the suffering. When she told her mother. She said "you decide Riti, its your life, your career" she said she want to go once. Ramya said okay.

Riti went there and she was doing well in her job. Everyday she would video call her mother and talk. One day she told that one of her office colleague proposed her for marriage and she too like him. Ramya agreed for marriage.

After 6 months Ramya noticed that Riti is not that happy, she is either avoiding talking to her or pretending that everything is alright. One day Ramya said "Riti, look, don't repeat the mistake i did. Nothing will happen to me, i will tolerate everything. I passed one of the worst phases of my life and you, my girl are ver very strong. So talk and tell me truth. Yes both should adjust in marriage but it should be from Both ends, not simply you are adjusting and he is dominating. Sit talk, find a middle way and if you don't feel that there's any solution then just come back, you are welcome always." And then Riti told that her husband was cheating on her and so she can't live with him anymore.

Ramya got one more shock but said "its okay beta, sometimes Shit happens. It happened and its over now. Forgive him for your mental peace so that you can forget him and move on"

Next 3 months were tough for them both. Emotional people are hurted most but when they bounce back, they come back with full energy. Riti came back and decided to open her Business. Ramya somewhere was blaming herself that she didn't took right decision for her daughter and so she was get these blank outs or she would sit and be lost in memories.

Next morning Riti got up made tea for her mother and coffee for herself and said "mom, stop blaming yourself. It was not anyone's fault. I chose him. I trusted him. And yes people make mistakes to learn. I learnt my lesson. Doesn't meaning will not trust anyone. I will. I will marry too when i will get person of my choice. So now my hero, you talk. Once you said talk Riti talk and resolve. Today i am telling you mom talk and share your load and be stress free"

Ramya looked at Riti proudly and said "ok ma'm as you say" and both of them laughed.

Sometimes listening to half or partly conversation creates a misunderstanding and sometimes it can lead you to pay a big amount. So better talk your heart out to your loved ones. They will listen and understand, rather tha you living in suffocation.

What will you do?

Garima proudly walk to the stage to receive her award on company's annual meeting day. She was one the hardworking employee and valuable asset to the company. Higher authorities liked her work and her boss too got recommendation of the dedicated work from the client. Few of her colleagues were jealous, which is common in every corporate or office culture. She was happy to get the credit of her hardwork that too in her dream company. She had come a long way to achieve this. She did it all by her own. All she had her knowledge, hardwork and talent with her. She took up the first job she got purely with her knowledge base because she was not privileged or having conatcts so that she can influence them or use some jack to get a job. She belonged to a common middle class family, where dreaming something big is not permitted, not because she is girl but because they can't afford.

When a girl is born in a middle class family, two things she gets by birth that are struggles and adjustments. She had done both in her childhood.

When she gave her first board and was confused what subjects to take in her higher secondary school, she was unaware what's coming her way, which is going to change her future.

She was waiting for her results and she didn't had much big aspirations. She was scholar in studies so, everyone in family hoped for good marks but there was not any pressure. And the result came, she hopes to get 90% but in one of her subject she got very low marks so her overall percentage fall down to 83%. But her parents were happy that she scored good marks. The schools were yet to open and she was enjoying her holidays. Her uncle came to visit her city for some work, so he came to meet her and the family. While having lunch everyone was sitting and uncle asked her boards percentage. Her father proudly told 83%. Uncle was quiet and then turned towards Garima and asked and what subjects are you thinking to take for higher studies? She said Science and smiled. Uncle was quiet again. They all finished lunch and she and her brother was helping mother to clean kitchen. Suddenly she overheard the conversation of her uncle and her father.

Uncle said "why is she taking science? What will she do taking science? Infact it will be very hard for you, brother. Science studiea are expensive, the school fee, the tuitions, and then college? What college she will go? Simple B.Sc. is not worth it. You understand and make her understand."

Father said "if she wish to take science, then we will let her do so. And you don't worey about expenses brother, i will manage. I have managed till date and further also i will manage."

Uncle said " you have a boy too, spare money for his studies, he is your asset for future. Why wasting money for Garima's studies?"

Father said "that's my worries. I will see what and how will i do. And Garima too is as important as our son. Why you made your daughter took science? If you are questioning my decision, you too have son."

Uncle said " i have a good decent job. I can manage my both kids graduation and post graduation studies and even job, but you, you my brother have an average business which make losses more than profit. So you should think carefully"

Father said "oh, thank you for the concern, but we take our family decisions mutually" and stood from there and went saying he has some meetings lined up with clients.

This whole conversation made a big impact on Garima. She was thinking about it day and night. She got into dilemma that whether i am putting financial pressure to my parents for the stream they can't afford for me? Or will i be able to go through the studies pressure and will able to get good marks? Constantly the words of her uncle and father were going on in her mind. So she went to her parents and said "what should i take sciencs or commerce or arts for further studies?"

Her mother said "arts? Where did it came from? You are a scholar student and you prooves it too by securing such good marks then why are you asking this? You only said science, you jave doubt now? Then you can take commerce? But your commercial maths is poor dear, i have taught you for years so i have idea about it. I think you will do better in science"

Her father qas quiet and looking in her eyes to find out what happened.

Garima listening to her mother said ok and went inside. Once again that uncle and father conversation tape played in her mind but this time, she made her mind and said to herself "uncle asked what will i do taking science, i will show him, what i will do. Also i will minimize the expenses as much as i can from my end to support parents and not to put a financial burden to them."

Those words as if gave her unmatched strength to fight all the odds coming in her way.

She worked hard and used to study thoroughly. She passed senior secondary boards with distinction and not only this she passed competition enterance exam with good score where she was able to get a good architecture college.

When she made it through such touch competition, she parents were happy. Now they had to worry for the college fee. In those 5 years she did all the hard work to study well and get herself a good job as she was studying on education loan. She wanted that before her parents start asking about marriage she gets a job and return all the loan amount. She got placed from the college placement. Her hardword paid well. She chose to struggle but not to compromise for less in those years.

Soon with her dedicated work she got recognition in her professional career. She switched in companies to get better opportunities. Finally she was able to repay the education loan and make her parents burden free. She even supported them for her brother studies.

After 5, today one of the popular company of the country has rewarded her for her qualified work and supreme designs.

When she stood on stage to receive the award she remembered her uncle's word that what she will do taking science? Today was her day to let him see that what she has achieved with her own hardwork by not doubting and compromising. She said thank you to her company, her seniors, her family and God that she got this opportunity.

When she came home taking the award, she was welcomed by her parents and brother with full enthusiasm and joy. All of them very happy and thankful to God. That day she made a call to her uncle and said "thank you uncle, if you didn't said those words to my father, and i didn't have overheard that conversation then i might not have been where i am today. So i am grateful to you as well."

Uncle was feeling bad could only say "no dear, you just misunderstood". Before he could complete his statement Garima said "uncle, if i misunderstood, then also thank you, this misunderstanding changed my life" and she ended the call.

One should never under estimate others or misunderstand their will towards life.

Ankita Baheti

Qatar

CHAPTER NINE

Lockdown and girlfriend

It was the story during 2018 when corona yet to kock door of world and everyone is living normally. The Shray is a good looking person with pleasent personality. He used to be on social media lot of time and chats with unkown too. One fine day when he is searching someone on Facebook he got a nice girl named Mithilesh Sharma. She is healthy some more weight on her and doing Research in Delhi University-DU. Both started a chats with each other and likes each other company on vitual platform. They after chatting for few months came to some level up from chat to phone calls. Both shared their hobbies eating and drinking habits with each other. Being a Research Scholar at DU she got habit of drinking alcohol and Shray too had same habits like her. Both talked on various topics and slowly they get into deeper and closer. Shray and her talk wbout menstrual cycle-mc and the paid she is facing during mc, the Shray was informed that the girl during MC used to tell that she is down instead of periods or having MC. This is very new information for him. Once there were no body at home of Shray and the days are of winter. The Shray told her to come to his home and meet him. She accepted the proposal and they scheduled time and date for meeting. As that was their first meeitng both were too excited for meeting. Slowly days passed and the date of meeting came on its way. Shray became ready to pick her up and she gave time of 1 PM Shray instructed her to wear winter jacket cover the head so that everyone in society feel that she is a boy.

Before she arrive at metro Shray too Whisky, Beer, Paneer Tikka and started waiting for her. When she arrived both greeted each other and they came to home. Shray becoming too excited to meet her, offered drinking water and aksed if she need drinks now. She answered that not now we will talk for some time then we will take. Shray started smooching to her and they both enjoyed each other on bed. After that Shray asked her what she like to drink then to her answer Shray too became amazed she demanded for cocktail of Whishky+Beer+Water. So accordingly Shray made a peg for her and for himself some sort fo beer. The cocktail worked well and she soon become drowned in drunken stage. Now after finish of first peg they again started making love and this time as usual the rlationship ran for more than 40 minutes. Both were puspirated in nude stage in winter. They felt awesome and their first meeting was over 2-3 more rounds.

After she had some conciousness then she requested to drop her in evening. As the winter days were there there is darnkness early so there were no problem to hide her and to drop her.

She left and Shray too came back home. The memories embarked in both minds for forever like markings created in stone which is permanent. They again became phone friends and chats on whatsapp. They ususally talks about Research and more and more about each other. The corona slowly came in society and when all were locked slowly no body guessed. The first wave gone then second wave went up and vaccination drive in India saved many lives. Touch wood the Mithilesh and Shray did not catched any infection during the period of corona. After the corona was over they again decided to meet but this time meeting will be outdoor stay for 3 days atleast. Mithilesh told that her brother and family will visit Goa and hence she told she will come before 3 days and stay with Shray and then join his brother and family. To her offer Shray became happy and she told Shray to do all expenses but wihtout worry she will pay her part later. So Shray happily booked tickets for both for Goa.

On date of journey they met in the Airport and by air they reached Goa. The Shray becoming a money savy person booked a budget hotel. Next morning Shray took a bike on rent and both of them after bathing and one round of meeting went for roaming to Panaji. The driving of Shray is safe while that of Mithilesh is too unsafe. She used to take long turn while turning the two whceler. They both somehow reach back to guest house drink some alcohol and after dinner slept together. Next morning they planed for visit to near by beach. Next early morning both of them went to nearby beach the Bambolim Beach. The quality of Beach is that its like a big swimming pool as water all strucked due to triangle beach shape. The Shray knows swimming hence he enjoyed swimming for 1-2 hours. Then they came to two wheeler parking to return to Guest House. Mithilesh demanded for driving to her demand Shray accepted. This time just fater start of ride as usual she take a long turning and both of them falled and had accident. As mithilesh was driving her one leg had injured more while Shray one leg had injury but not that extent.

Now some how Shray managed to drive two wheeler and both came back to Guest House. Shray went to nearby hospital and baought some First Aids. After coming to Guest House he gave First Aid to Mithilesh. After 2-3 hours both wake up and they were feeling far better. Now they had almost 2 days in hand and nothing to visit because of injuries.

So Shray used to remove her panty only from one leg used to make relation and then redress her. This continued for next 2 days or say 20 times. both enjoyed sex in pain and pain in sex.

After coming back as predicted by Shray she did not gave any expenses sharing and this become a cause of miss-understanding between them. They lived together they become away with their career pathways ahead.

Sachin C Narwadiya

Ghaziabad

Credit: https://pixabay.com/

CHAPTER TEN

What will you do?

Garima proudly walk to the stage to receive her award on company's annual meeting day. She was one the hardworking employee and valuable asset to the company. Higher authorities liked her work and her boss too got recommendation of the dedicated work from the client. Few of her colleagues were jealous, which is common in every corporate or office culture. She was happy to get the credit of her hardwork that too in her dream company. She had come a long way to achieve this. She did it all by her own. All she had her knowledge, hardwork and talent with her. She took up the first job she got purely with her knowledge base because she was not privileged or having conatcts so that she can influence them or use some jack to get a job. She belonged to a common middle class family, where dreaming something big is not permitted, not because she is girl but because they can't afford.

When a girl is born in a middle class family, two things she gets by birth that are struggles and adjustments. She had done both in her childhood.

When she gave her first board and was confused what subjects to take in her higher secondary school, she was unaware what's coming her way, which is going to change her future.

She was waiting for her results and she didn't had much big aspirations. She was scholar in studies so, everyone in family hoped for good marks but there was not any pressure. And the result came, she hopes to get 90% but in one of her subject she got very low marks so her overall percentage fall down to 83%. But her parents were happy that she scored good marks. The schools were yet to open and she was enjoying her holidays. Her uncle came to visit her city for some work, so he came to meet her and the family. While having lunch everyone was sitting and uncle asked her boards percentage. Her father proudly told 83%. Uncle was quiet and then turned towards Garima and asked and what subjects are you thinking to take for higher studies? She said Science and smiled. Uncle was quiet again. They all finished lunch and she and her brother was helping mother to clean kitchen. Suddenly she overheard the conversation of her uncle and her father.

Uncle said "why is she taking science? What will she do taking science? Infact it will be very hard for you, brother. Science studiea are expensive, the school fee, the tuitions, and then college? What college she will go? Simple B.Sc. is not worth it. You understand and make her understand."

Father said "if she wish to take science, then we will let her do so. And you don't worey about expenses brother, i will manage. I have managed till date and further also i will manage."

Uncle said " you have a boy too, spare money for his studies, he is your asset for future. Why wasting money for Garima's studies?"

Father said "that's my worries. I will see what and how will i do. And Garima too is as important as our son. Why you made your daughter took science? If you are questioning my decision, you too have son."

Uncle said " i have a good decent job. I can manage my both kids graduation and post graduation studies and even job, but you, you my brother have an average business which make losses more than profit. So you should think carefully"

Father said "oh, thank you for the concern, but we take our family decisions mutually" and stood from there and went saying he has some meetings lined up with clients.

This whole conversation made a big impact on Garima. She was thinking about it day and night. She got into dilemma that whether i am putting financial pressure to my parents for the stream they can't afford for me? Or will i be able to go through the studies pressure and will able to get good marks? Constantly the words of her uncle and father were going on in her mind. So she went to her parents and said "what should i take sciencs or commerce or arts for further studies?"

Her mother said "arts? Where did it came from? You are a scholar student and you prooves it too by securing such good marks then why are you asking this? You only said science, you jave doubt now? Then you can take commerce? But your commercial maths is poor dear, i have taught you for years so i have idea about it. I think you will do better in science"

Her father qas quiet and looking in her eyes to find out what happened.

Garima listening to her mother said ok and went inside. Once again that uncle and father conversation tape played in her mind but this time, she made her mind and said to herself "uncle asked what will i do taking science, i will show him, what i will do. Also i will minimize the expenses as much as i can from my end to support parents and not to put a financial burden to them."

Those words as if gave her unmatched strength to fight all the odds coming in her way.

She worked hard and used to study thoroughly. She passed senior secondary boards with distinction and not only this she passed competition enterance exam with good score where she was able to get a good architecture college.

When she made it through such touch competition, she parents were happy. Now they had to worry for the college fee. In those 5 years she did all the hard work to study well and get herself a good job as she was studying on education loan. She wanted that before her parents start asking about marriage she gets a job and return all the loan amount. She got placed from the college placement. Her hardword paid well. She chose to struggle but not to compromise for less in those years.

Soon with her dedicated work she got recognition in her professional career. She switched in companies to get better opportunities. Finally she was able to repay the education loan and make her parents burden free. She even supported them for her brother studies.

After 5, today one of the popular company of the country has rewarded her for her qualified work and supreme designs.

When she stood on stage to receive the award she remembered her uncle's word that what she will do taking science? Today was her day to let him see that what she has achieved with her own hardwork by not doubting and compromising. She said thank you to her company, her seniors, her family and God that she got this opportunity.

When she came home taking the award, she was welcomed by her parents and brother with full enthusiasm and joy. All of them very happy and thankful to God. That day she made a call to her uncle and said "thank you uncle, if you didn't said those words to my father, and i didn't have overheard that conversation then i might not have been where i am today. So i am grateful to you as well."

Uncle was feeling bad could only say "no dear, you just misunderstood". Before he could complete his statement Garima said "uncle, if i misunderstood, then also thank you, this misunderstanding changed my life" and she ended the call.

One should never under estimate others or misunderstand their will towards life.

Ankita Baheti

Qatar

Credit: https://pixabay.com/

Printed by Libri Plureos GmbH in Hamburg,
Germany